Garlic Mustard

by Stray B. Frankenstein

To the younger me
who never thought they would live
to escape this pain

Table of Contents

February 4th

before I met you, I was so alone
love was something entirely unknown

yet now, I feel it inside me
blooming like the apple tree

that we swore to meet under
come rain or come thunder

though it's too early to see its glorious flowers
I feel it will bloom soon, like this love of ours

we swore to meet here before we go
for you had a confession you wanted me to know

though it was unspoken before
I knew the reason you asked to meet for

though your mouth was silent
your actions were defiant

expressing that which you were too nervous to say
as your rosy cheeks put it on display

now as the dying sun tints the world ruby
all I can think of is your beauty

slowly, I watch you make your way
up to where I feel like I've waited all day

my heart stops in its tracks
as I'm suddenly unable to relax

seeing you here with me now
makes me wonder how

anyone as divine
would want to be mine

your confession brings me to tears
as the dying sun all but disappears

and you set my heart ablaze
as I watch you bask in crimson rays

February 5th

even as night gives way to dawn
I still can't get you out of my mind
you've left it scrambled
unable to think through love's haze
sleep evades me as I relive yesterday
— our first date
relief and joy wash over me in waves
flowing without ebbing
submerging me in adoration's sea

February 6th

To Flow Without Ebbing

join me in love's light
bask in its healing rays
leave behind your sorrow and spite
peak out through anger's haze
float with me in peaceful tranquility
join me in love's sea
let this feeling stretch into infinity
feel what it really means to be

February 7th

take my hand
and I'll take yours
walk with me
through the garden
of divine ecstasy
pass by all that is forbidden
dangerous and tantalizing
refuse their beguiling pleasures
and stay by my side

February 8th

though our time together
has not yet proven lasting
I've made a place for you
in the center of my heart
a room just for you
where the furniture is not yet worn
and it lacks a homey feel
but in time
once you've settled in
we can wear it in together
smile fondly at every tear and mark
with the memory of its creation
held close to our hearts

February 9th

you're so cruel
leaving when we've just started
going out of your way to get me
just to bring me back again
time with you is never enough
it runs too fast
escaping when my heart's at its fullest
leaving me alone when I want you most
the promise of seeing you again keeps me going
but I know that time will slow in your absence
and frantically flee again
the moment our eyes meet

February 10th

as I wake in your absence
the morning lacks balance
without your smile to light up the room
not even the sun could cut through the gloom
though we were together just yesterday
for so long we almost ran out of things to say
I still miss you in this brief moment
as distance makes my love even more potent
though I'm too nervous now to gently hold your face
I know that one day, I'll be ready for that simple
embrace

February 11th

when the week has worn me thin
and fatigue has taken hold
you ignite a fire within
as my heart connects with yours of gold
revitalizing me with a single glance
snuck in during the lull of your conversation
your deep eyes sending me into a trance
though they do not approve of our affiliation
they find it cute that you make time
to show me that you care
for they know that love is no crime
and it's beautiful to lay it bare

February 12th

from early morning's stupor
I'm brought to attention by a familiar ring
you call, asking me about my future
quickly changing your question, you ask what tomorrow
will bring
I tell you I have nothing to do
to which you pitch your amorous scheme
you tell me about a lovely spot with a view
describing a date straight out of a dream
you confess to me all the love in your heart
and ask me to be your Valentine, please
I tell you that I'd love to, and I cannot bear to be apart
you tell me how this spot is surrounded in trees
how they have not yet bloomed
you wish you could force out their romantic flowers
for the clearing would be beautifully perfumed
and we could watch the petals fall for hours

as we giggle and laugh
I grow ever more grateful
that you get to be my other half

February 13th

the clock ticks away
working against me
as I sit here
ready and attentive
waiting on a promise
passing time by watching its hands
spin endlessly round
losing my faith
as time loses its meaning

February 14th

No Call No Show

hold it to the light
make it burn
hot as the hatred inside
hot as the anger and regret
swirling inside
stare into the sun
to blind yourself to unfortunate truth
as you continue to love

February 15th

yesterday's anger disappears in a flash
its fire reduced to ash
the moment we meet eye to eye
I dare not question why
you left me high and dry
without so much as a reply
to all the messages I sent
asking what your absence meant

with a smile
I asked you to stay a while
so that your lips can apologize without sound

February 16th

the world lies dormant
as nature holds its breath
silently awaiting
the return of spring
and its floral tide

February 17th

as the temperature swings low
my emotions swing ever higher
cutting through sorrow's snow
melting it with red hot desire
warming the frozen ground beneath
ending winter's sadness unusually early
it can no longer bare its frozen teeth

February 18th

the flowers will always be remembered
though the winter washes them away
they always resurface
brief winter cannot erase
the memory of months
full of their beautiful blooms
but when I die
when the aging winter washes me out
I won't return in the spring
once the tides change
how will I be remembered
if my death is eternal?

February 19th

heal me with your delicate hands
ground me with your soothing voice
hold me while I weep
keep me safe even in my darkest hour
stay with me
bathe me in love's light
and wash away my woes

February 20th

your smile is my favorite surprise
as I open the door with half shut eyes
tired annoyance turning into unbridled glee
it's a blessing that you're the first person I see
after tossing and turning in a half conscious haze
kept away from the sun's newborn rays
which I am now flung into
as I leave to get brunch with you

February 21st

I stumbled upon the most glorious sight
as I walked in the sun's light
a delicate flower
that awakened a magnificent power
the ability to break out of winter's haze
to punch through it and live out my days
to the fullest extent possible
to finish that which I once thought impossible
to carry on with my daily chore
of writing poetry about what the day had in store
but now I do it without hesitation
tending to this journal with the utmost attention
carrying it with me wherever I go
knowing that I can never truly know
when inspiration will find me
it could strike regardless of when or where I happen to
be

the final nail in the coffin of winter woes
hammered in by the first flower after it snows

February 22nd

our late night calls
have become the best part of my routine
and my only concern as I walk these halls
I now find myself getting nightly caffeine
to extend our time before I fall asleep
but eventually it catches up to me
I get to listen to your voice as I go to sleep
there's no way I'd rather it be

February 23rd

I see you every time I close my eyes
for with you there are no permanent goodbyes
despite the distance between us
we are never out of things to discuss
day and night we talk and talk
and with each word you steadily unlock
the door to my heart's core
where I want you to stay forevermore

February 24th

I walk beneath skeletons everyday
with the memory of how they used to sway
when they were adorned in leafy flesh
and the light gently filtered through their mesh

February 25th

I see you in every shadow
and in every ray of light
I hear you in the call of every sparrow
and in nature's song at night
the world carries you with me
when you're not here
though I'd rather you be
with me right here

February 26th

today as I follow you out
I cannot help but look about
to look at every wall
and admire how the ivy stands tall
consuming that which used to be pristine
marring it and never letting it be clean
it will be scarred with its unrelenting invasion
permanently marked by its domination

as I look into your eyes and see the ivy's reflection
the beckoning green that marks manipulation
I wonder what the difference is between man and ivy

February 27th

tonight I'll sleep alone
I can't bring myself to pick up the phone
it rings and rings
but I know what it brings
uncertainty and plastic promises
as you tell me I remind you of goddesses
perfectly carved marble statues
which tell me your true values
that the flesh outweighs the brain
that to be loved is to be vain

February 28th

when can I be clean?
no amount of time or soap can wash it away
it has clung to me for far too long
I was too young to understand
to grasp what happened
but now that I do
I can't forget again
I can't push it away again to protect myself
it's here and now and it won't leave
the mud has left but it left stains
and I will carry them until the Earth takes me

March 1st

every second spent apart
drives stakes in my heart
with every call late at night
I yearn more and more to live in your heart's light

March 2nd

from my heart's tower
fly the crows
the vultures
the buzzards
feasting on the carrion
littered around the barren field
the stench unbearable
worsening as they approach
the spiked walls
which lay waste to the unworthy
who try to climb over
my heart's walls
to conquer the world within

March 3rd

I miss the flowers
delicately adorning the fields
blooming for a few precious hours
the most divine of nature's yields
I wish we could dance in them together
frolic joyfully among them
embrace in the altogether

March 4th

as I invite you into my room
I see your eyes widen at the sight
they slowly adjust to the gloom
and I open the curtains to the sun's light
everything here is new to you
you're too new in my life to know
about this place where I grew
you've never seen the morning's glow
shine through to light the room
illuminating the dust's ancient dance
while they wander in childhood's tomb

as I look at you now
I realize your ears are empty
they don't ring with childhood's echo
while mine are consumed by it

March 5th

your eyes are my favorite sight
delicately glowing when they hit the light
meeting them will always make my heart
stop and start
as I melt into your chest
knowing that you're the best
lover I could ever hope for

March 6th

as I delicately paint the sky
and wash my canvas in blue
I can't help but smile and wonder why
all I can think about is you
nature's elegant beauty
has begun to feel like an echo of you

March 7th

fog has settled in my mind
diluting my thoughts
removing from them all meaning
hollowing them out
and leaving me with husks
I put them inside each other
to try and complete them
only to leave them
more scattered than I found them

March 8th

I'll forever crave your attention
your everlasting care and devotion
I'd wait as long as I needed
as day and night I've pleaded
prayed to bright stars and invisible gods
that our love could defy all odds
exist in spite of hatred and dissent
survive through life's unrelenting torment
make it out on the other side
together no matter how much we cried
knowing that despite it all
our love will always stand tall

March 9th

the deer is always seen as weak
defenseless and meek
naïve, an easy target
innocence incarnate
but they've never seen them fight
protect against a vicious bite
stamping them into the ground
disarming them without a sound
as they carry on without a care
always prepared to fight against those who dare
to destroy that which they view
as defenseless without a clue

March 10th

I wish I could buy you the world
serve it to you on a silver platter
deliver you your every desire
make your every dream a reality
for that's what you deserve
to live in divine ecstasy
to enjoy it to the fullest extent
live without struggle or worry
for you've suffered too much already
and I'd happily die a thousand deaths
for you to live a day without pain

March 11th

I'm addicted to the taste of your lips
their intoxicating cherry flavor
pulling me in like a siren
singing her ballad for a sailor
pulling their boat into rocky shallows
so that they may join her collection
of wrecked ships and broken hearts

March 12th

with your breathe hot on my neck
and your hands holding me tight
you've turned me into an emotional wreck
holding back tears of joy and delight
for months I've dreamed of your now casual embrace
holding myself and smiling at the feeling
praying that one day our fingers would interlace
so my heart could finally start healing

now that we're finally here
finally where I dreamed we'd be
I find myself remembering the deer
prancing in fields wild and free
without a care in the world
besides which flower to taste next
as I survey those with petals pearled
finally free to live unvexed

March 13th

the world has begun to wear on me
eroding my soul as the road does tires
slowly sanding them bear
losing traction
losing the will to go on
fear propels me forward
as well as my daily goal
one a day seems to small
but as I see these pages swell
with the words of my love and hate
I wonder what will become of it
once the weeds take me
dragging me through the soil

will this be all I'm remembered for?
erased from the minds of those I've known
I sit here in eerie silence
contemplating who they'll picture me as
once I'm only bone
and this diary is all that's left
tucked away collecting dust
on my life's bookshelf

March 14th

walking from brook to brook
embracing nature's radiating warmth
happily observing where she retook
man made ruins as life springs forth
cracking through concrete
and running up the walls
refusing to admit defeat
at the hands of primitive dolls
thinking they're above their creator
as they replace her with man made origin
pretending they never came from nature

March 15th

beautiful flowers
decorate my afternoon stroll
as I dance among stalks tall as towers
their roots extend into my soul
connecting me to stalks and earth
blurring the line between human and animal
preparing me for divine rebirth
yet I feel a pull barely tangible
tethering me to humanity
pulling me away from the divine
a budding seed hanging with impressive tenacity
sprouting from my head and spine
invading and conquering my vulnerable mind
binding me to a tree that will never bloom

March 16th

your voice whispers to me
in your absence
it echoes around my skull
overshadowing any conscious thought
at first a welcome distraction
from deafening silence
but now it's destroying me
tearing me apart
as it runs in circles
banging around my head
as headaches ravage me
your voice grows so strong
I hear bone shatter

March 17th

invite me into your heart
open it up to my perspective
see the world as the finest art
view the world as a collective
please, see me eye to eye
change your mind for even a day
for me would you at least try
to see the world in more than just grey
expose yourself to life's vibrant spectrum
before you judge me for living in it

March 18th

does change go both ways
will you change as I do
while I embrace your ways
open myself up to something new
try to view all in shades of grey
I fear you're draining life's hues
steadily leading me astray
forcing me to choose
between my truth and yours
between my own future or one forced

March 19th

I now dread seeing you
though I'm hopelessly in love
I no longer know what it means to be true
for your everlasting unlove
has planted in me seeds
that now tether me to you
and your mental weeds
I no longer know what to do
as you take root in my brain
imbedding yourself in its maze

March 20th

gravel crunches underfoot
while I stride confidently
towards you
swallowing my pride
as I pretend we're fine
my heart defies me
swelling as we kiss
pulling me back towards you

maybe I imagined our problems
inventing them to explain my woes
right now we're okay
in love in the purest way

please, I pray to all that will listen
let our problems exist only in my imagination

March 21st

with hands desperately clasped together
I whisper a plea to the divine
propelling my message into the ether
doing all I can to keep us fine
and melt away my overreactive fears
as I learn to love the sprouting seed
that snuck in through my ears

March 22nd

I wish I was free
living in constant glee
free to roam as I please
running through the trees
prancing with the deer
leaving behind all fear
adopting nature and she adopts me

March 23rd

I beg the stars to return my energy
it's been taken from my soul
taken away to feed
this invasive seed
I can feel its strengthening pulse
as it steals mine
as its roots sneak down my spine
stretching outwards
to twist around my bones

please dear god
let the deer eat me

March 24th

rosettes have begun to sprout
beneath our apple tree
I think of pulling them out
despite not knowing what they may be
they're too small yet to tell
but I feel they're my parasite's twin
disgusting leafy disease from hell
that I feel wriggling in my skin

I seethe as I realize what's here
the garlic mustard has taken hold
knowing it won't be touched by the deer
I quickly grasp hold
of young stems
tearing them from their host

March 25th

I've learned to fear your touch
for with it you attach strings
to be kissed is to allow for more
though you tell me I can decline
your rampant advances
your eyes tell me a different story
whenever my shaken voice
dares to defy you
turning you down
they tell me that I've failed
a test I never knew I was taking

March 26th

will I ever be ready
to give myself up to you
tear off my clothes
and lay before you bare

you're so eager to touch me
I've started to think
it's all you want from me

March 27th

we walk hand in hand
down cracked sidewalks
effortlessly devoted
to one another

today I hold your hand
a little tighter
scared that it may be the last time
I get to love you like this

I feel change swirling around me
I fear it will come for us next
and sweep me out
from under my feet

March 28th

I want to feel power
the unbridled ability
to rule myself and my destiny

I need to take charge
of my life in decline
I need to leave behind
all that tethers me

I have no desire to wait
on sprouting seeds

I'm afraid of what's happening
to me and those around me
the world is bending
pushing and pulling
ebbing and flowing at my feet

the divine has reached me
embedded itself in me
where stem meets spine
I feel it reaching through me
twisting around my internal structure

call off the deer
they no longer see me
call the hounds
to devour me

March 29th

I watch the walls melt
and the moss grow
from underneath
as it dies and turns back
to that which it once was

I watch it live and die
melt and flow
move and breathe
float up and down
the wall it sprouts from

I reach out and graze it
sink into it
and fall further beyond

March 30th

time slows
to a screeching stop
as I watch the world
refuse to turn
leaving me to rust
as I wait in the future
for the past to reach me

March 31st

windows turn to doors
as doors turn to windows
neither will budge
holding me in a cell
showing me the key to salvation
and hiding it away again
teasing me as I watch
my leafy assassin sprout
through windows
and under doors
reaching for limbs
ready to embrace them
as chlorophyll replaces the blood
pumping through my infested heart

April 1st

I adopted nature and she rejected me
filling me with man eating vines
it eats through me
replaces me
tears through me

I feel it attacking me
breaking and reforming
my fragile skeleton

what did I do
to warrant this violence?

April 2nd

stones settle
in my soles
dragging me down
towards rocky bottom

kelp shivers in the current
raging back and forth
wrapping around me
as I fall

the sharks won't eat me
for I'm too tainted to be eaten

the eels pay me no mind
for I'm too tainted to be eaten

the crabs scurry away
for I'm too tainted to be eaten

they watch as I drown
refusing to end my suffering
for I'm too tainted to be eaten

April 3rd

I can't accept your touch
it's too delicate
for me to bear
it lures me closer to you
calms me for a while
but I'm afraid
of what I'll do to you
when I've awaken from my trance

you know I'm horrible
I see it in your eyes
I see the fear erupt
with every sound I make

you know I'm too tainted to be loved
yet you try anyway
knowing you can never love me
you hold me like you do
talk to me like you do
pretend like you do
I love you, but I'm scared
I'll look into your eyes one day
and only see my reflection
painted in the sun's light
instead of rose

April 4th

I know now why the sun burns
she hates her creation
day and night she yearns
for their destruction
she prays to nature and the moon
to wipe us out as we rest
I pray that one day soon
she can finally rest
as she watches our lifeless bodies
refuse to come back again

April 5th

from my heart's
highest cliff
I see the fog
it trembles and breathes
shuddering
with every step
I watch the birds
soar through it
tearing it apart
as I plummet towards it
I beg for forgiveness
praying that nature
will invite me with open arms
and grant me quick mercy

April 6th

do the gods watch down
upon their tiny creations
and think of us
the way we think of ants?

do they feel shame
when they decimate our cities

do they topple us by accident
the way we do ant hills
running over them
squashing their only exit
because we're too big to notice
too big to care?

April 7th

the forest speaks
in words we can't hear
a language meant
only for nature's true children
it screams for us to halt
rethink our industrial disposition
their words will never reach us
for they echo through empty halls
resonating only with their speakers

the world is screaming
we see its frantic act
but we ignore it
as we ignore the silent
and we meet it
only with more violence

April 8th

to live is to murder
to live is to die
life and death are one and the same
locked in a perpetual cycle
of destroying the other

they come for all of us
life sustains us
as death feeds us
for no food exists
without the death of another

I feel death all around me
as my body rots
a sprout has grown inside me
and it sucks away my life
cutting me out from the cycle
delivering me straight to death

April 9th

I watch the world erupt
in nature's beautiful colors
bloom all around me
yet now as I need it most
I can't enjoy its beauty
nature planted in me
my own destruction
and now I can no longer
enjoy her endless blessings
as I feel my parasite
take control of my mortal body
and lie on my undug grave
waiting for my beloved
to dig it out from under me

April 10th

did the dinosaurs know
that they were moments from extinction
as the meteor closed in
and cooked them alive

as they hid from its heat
did they understand
the gravity of the situation
did they know
that everyone was dying with them
or did they feel alone
isolated
scared like a child in a dark room

am I dying alone
or has this seed
infected the bodies of others
will we know
if we are truly alone
before the lights go out

April 11th

I cross my heart
with twin blades
nicking it
as I squeeze the shears
I smell the forest
while green blood
flows from my open chest

hands shake
unable to close the shears
and close the book of my life

I'm a prisoner in my own body
and there is no key to my cell
for the only escape is annihilation

April 12th

bring forth the deer
I need them near
they bring succor
and save me from her
from nature's great wrath
and lead me down a path
towards brighter days
but I now know there's several ways
to gain the trust of your prey
and so now I pray
that they'll be merciful
and my end won't be painful
as I'm trampled by my own naïveté

April 13th

I fall from life's tower
plunging into foggy death
time dilates here
slowing as I fall
the once close fog
is now a lifetime away
a lifetime I no longer want
for this seed has taken all
it needs me to survive
but I can't live with it
I'd kill myself
to take away this pain

April 14th

as the world caves in
crashing around me
I'm left only with you
and your loving touch
hold me through the night
keep the dark at bay
life in your absence
is cruel and perilous
but with you
I see the light
breaking through
sorrow's void

April 15th

everything comes from something
yet
this seed came from nothing
I will never know where this threat
inherited its fangs
I will never know
I'm left alone
in an endless void
with only this sprout
growing down my spine
my only ally
and my biggest threat

I see it in your eyes' reflection
and your fake meek smile
oh dear god
please
find me another answer

April 16th

I hide myself from the light
for a sprout will die without it
it beckons me forward
promises me love and hope
but I know that once I give in
this parasite
will spring back to life
eating me away
as I reach out desperately
towards crimson rays

April 17th

please help me
let my words
bring you to me
though you may never read them
please
let them find you
through the ether
rid me of this terrible seed
and take away my fear
that you planted it
for I know deep down
you never would

I'm begging you
please tell me
that you never could

April 18th

see me in front of you
look past my damage
past the knicks and scratches
look into my mind
find the source
of my malfunction
and tear it out

fix me
even if it means destroying me
I trust you to rebuild me

April 19th

I can no longer enjoy the flowers
they've betrayed me and left me
to die without their presence
they sold me to the smog
and told it exactly
how to ruin me

I watch as they dance
in the gentle breeze
as tears begin falling
down my warm cheeks

how could something so beautiful
do something this heinous to me?

April 20th

sorrow's fog lifts momentarily
as I bask in new light
delightfully warm
it fills me with comfort
enveloping me like a blanket
lulling me towards
gentle sleep
removing the burden
of life's struggles
only for a moment
but this feeling
transcends time
as it distorts around it
flowing indecisively
it knows not where it's going
it just knows it's going
somewhere eventually
if it keeps shifting
maybe it will find
this fabled place

April 21st

fog closes in once more
as pleasure dissipates
leaving me in the dark
without my new light
a new path to salvation
now lost to me
for the key has left my hands
and I can no longer
open its glowing gate

April 22nd

white pearls
sit atop stalks
with pointed leaves
they bloom out of spite
of the tree they sit beneath
whose branches remain nearly bare
as the leaves all but refuse to return
starving it of the sun's glorious light
and forcing it to watch those glowing flowers
blossoming and thriving beneath its living skeleton

April 23rd

my heart grows thorns
pinching and piercing it
destroying that which it adorns
as it squeezes, refusing to fit
turning itself from a protective cage
to an iron maiden
killing its host in its rage
as blood flows out of the laden
dripping down onto sprouting leaves
and beading as morning dew

April 24th

hold me close
I haven't much time
for in me grows
the sprouting seed
made to destroy me
it eats through my brain
leaving me an empty shell

if you won't pull it out
hold me in my final moments
before death takes me
and my corpse is reanimated
by my opposite

April 25th

it will never be enough
to only see you
in these fleeting moments
I live and breath
for your presence and touch
everyday has become a countdown
until we get to lie together again
laughing and giggling
as we take in the other's beauty
and pray that every second
could be just like this

April 26th

butterflies give themselves to the wind
living freely away from all worry
they're too pure to have sinned
they're free from the hurry
to atone for existing
and embracing that existence
no one is behind them twisting
every thought into blasphemous resistance

as the steady breeze whirls around me
I wish I could give myself to the wind

April 27th

walk through my silent heart
wander its halls
find comfort in its warmth
lose yourself
as I'm losing myself
set fire to my heart
so I may follow its light
and find myself again

April 28th

our tree is still not in bloom
does it mean we're destined for doom?
does this tree dictate our future?
sewing us together with divine suture
connecting the fabric of our lives
ensuring that our love survives

maybe it's the other way around
that our love must travel underground
through its roots to nourish it
watching it bloom as we commit
to each other and swear
that despite the world's wear
we will forever belong to each other
and forever remain together

April 29th

your voice masks my own
I know hear it in my every word
you're changing me
molding me to be like you
will I lose myself in you?

to be loved is to be changed
permanently altered
but does the same go for you?
do you change as I do?
or am I changing
to better fit you
while you change me
to avoid changing yourself

April 30th

eyes sparkle
in the dimming light
your face
painted in shades of gold
as the sun sinks
below the horizon

it scares me how beautiful you are
illuminated by death's shadow

May 1st

beasts lurk in the ether
preying on vulnerable souls
distorting our pleas
to the divine
they've followed my soul
back to its host
they take pity on me
for they've found the seed
planted within
even the most vicious beasts
refuse to hurt me
for I've already fallen victim
to a predator
far greater than them

May 2nd

I see the light at the end of the tunnel
the promise of momentary freedom
I stand before it
exhilarated and afraid
I hate my current routine
as much as I love it
I feel comforted knowing
that every day
has a purpose
a goal I can look at and understand
I fear I'll fall apart without it
it holds me together
when I lose direction
though I know this freedom
is brief
ending as soon as it begins
but even a moment
without something to hold me together
might leave me too lost
to embrace it again

May 3rd

hold me together
with your vices
let constant disrespect
keep me whole
as I give myself over
to the one I trust the most
knowing that it could be the death of me

please
hold me together
with the flawed soul
I fell for

May 4th

take my shaking hands
and calm them with your words
tell me what I need to hear
whisper intoxicating lies
into my empty ears
I beg for your voice to resound in them
until time comes to
a screeching halt
and rips it from memory

May 5th

shame bites at my ankles
begging me to raise it
far above me
nurture it through my decaying days
let it consume me
as I grow closer
to the all consuming
while I run towards
my life's horizon
and throw myself
into the dying sun

May 6th

the roots reach for me
grabbing at my ankles
threatening to plunge me
into the rotting ground
throwing me back
into nature's decay
as I desperately flee
arms outstretched
begging for nature's invitation
into the realm of the living

May 7th

let the weeds grow
up around your ankles
anchor you to the warm soil
let the dappled sunlight
rain down upon you
and bask in its glory
treasure these scared moments
in nature's reign
before you're ripped
from her loving arms
once more

May 8th

the love of the forest
ebbs and flows
as an erratic, emotional tide
threatening to swallow me
in waves of consuming love
and engulfing hatred
vibes wrap around my legs
waiting for the right moment
to drag me out
into unknown waters

May 9th

I stand on the edge of nature and man
unsure which side will welcome me
I've been burned before
and I will be burned again
but this time
this time will be different
now I know
I know the cruelty of nature
and the cruelty of man
I know which is kinder
but still
I'm standing here
unable to move
I need nature
I need to bask in her beauty
but the wound's still bleeding

will I be forever stuck
unable to forgive
the one I know I need?

May 10th

my mind wanders an endless plane
praying that it will find an answer here
the seed follows close behind
corrupting me from my shadow
will I ever find a way to be free
no matter which side I choose
one of us will suffer
one of us will force the other to suffer too
the seed pulls me back towards man
and their industrial filth
while I'm tearing myself apart
trying to return to nature
so that I may purge myself of this parasite
and return to how I once was
return to how I'm destined to be

May 11th

I beg him to come and rescue me
save me from my prison
take me away
deliver me from my sorrows
and ignite my life with adoration
I beg him to come and he swears he will
yet he never has
he swears and swears
and yet
I'm still here
moss has taken hold on my small space
growing on every corner
the light hits it so perfectly
that it nearly glows
the same color as the ivy
I once saw reflected in your eyes

May 12th

time drags on
as I lay here
stagnant
unable to free myself
from sorrow's solitude
when will your memory
be enough
when will I be able to live
without your constant touch

I can no longer tell
if this love
is a blessing or curse

May 13th

I miss you now
more than you'd ever allow
my heart aches for you
no matter what you do
I'm lost without your gaze
guiding me through my days
saving me from myself
from the horrors of the self
I beg you to take away my choice
take over and become my voice
I need you to decide
which is the better side
for us and not for me
I will choose whichever you claim it to be

May 14th

pain shoots from old wounds
breaking me apart
I feel it
burrowing further in
eating away at my skin
implanting itself in every corner
of my rotting body
please dear god
take away man's cruelty
take away this budding seed
filled with nothing but a lover's greed
please save me
before the seed takes me

May 15th

the days drag me out
threatening to unravel
the delicate threads of time
I see the world around me
through different eyes now
I see the change
that's taken hold
I've lost myself
to this force
the mirror no longer shows me
for I've forgotten how I look

I pray for a savior
to delivery me from this change
save me from that which ails me
free me from the shackles
of the force forcing this upon me

May 16th

I see your face
through mind's fog
glowing against
the dark unknown
I run towards you
yet you retreat faster

will I finally be free
from this turmoil and regret
when I give myself
up to you
let you take the wheel
of my fate and future

May 17th

the storm rages on
soaking me in boiling rain
I hear the thunder crack
I see the lightning strike
and I stand here unafraid
none of this is real
this is the seed
it's trying to force me
to cry
to scream
to beg you for mercy
I will brave the storm
and come back ready
dry and ready
as I send a storm
through your heart
before I tear it out
so you may feel
the pain you've made me feel

May 18th

with newfound resolve
I sit and wait
unraveling the threads of my mind
unraveling the quilt
of loving memory
I'm ready now
to strike like lightning
and deafen like thunder
I will enact this revenge
or I will die
lose myself to you and die
I know now that you did this to me
implanted in me this leeching seed
and feigned ignorance at my decline

I pray for the strength
to take nature's side
and destroy you
the cruel man
who burnt down
my heart's forest

May 19th

I sharpen my mind
against whetstone
readying it
to tear through
the fabric of your mind
so that I may expose
the threads holding it together
and pull them out
unraveling you
and your menacing influence

May 20th

the future races towards me
like the wind racing through the trees
and the shark race
with mouths wide open
towards their prey
I see it laid before me
threatening to swallow me whole
I see what will happen
and I see what could happen
the world has laid itself in front of me
as a myriad of possibilities
and my heart races towards his future
but my mind pulls back
racing towards my own
severing the connection between the two
and leading me to walk
on both sides of possibility

May 21st

the wind has lost its sound
flowing silently
through human husk
eroding the delicate casing
holding back the flood
threatening to drown
my beloved
for though they made these waters
they would never swim
guilt and shame
would shackle their ankles
anchoring them
to watery fate

May 22nd

the world has lost its hum
I fear it's gone numb
tired of singing its tune
in the face of impending doom
letting silence fall
as the hounds maul
my body now still
for I have lost the will
to fight against this seed
as I continually bleed
day and night
without the will to fight
and save my frail mind
from that which lurks behind
the facade of love and desire

May 23rd

I can feel the emerging evil
finally leave its shell
hatching
already baring its fangs
prepared to strike
at the innocent
unrelenting cruelty
is sure to follow
in its destructive wake

May 24th

from love's disruption
the seed sprung forth
I know where it came from
and where it's going
but this egg
the hatching of evil
and the release
of this oppressive aura
I know not where it came from
nor where it's going
this uncertainty threatens
to tear me to pieces

I pray that I'm safe from the birth of evil
but I know
I know it will find me
I know it will leave me on blackened sand
where the tide will take me
and hide me at the bottom of the sea
never to surface again

May 25th

I hide from the world
unable to repress my unending fear
I feel the evil
spreading
oh dear God please save me
I'd take the hounds over this
over this unending torment
please release me
from the shackles of fear
and let me soar once more
above it all

let me feel the manic ecstasy
so I can live again
for without the will to live
the evil will take me
and lure me down
to the wet, sandy bottom

May 26th

where has nature gone?
when did her glorious light
become overshadowed
by the ocean's blinding reflection?
where has she gone?

I stand here waiting for her return
eager to embrace her once more
but now
my arms fill with sand
instead of leaves
my wounds stinging with salt water
instead of healed and soothed
by nature's loving light

why must man
replace her
with the treacherous ocean?
replacing my gentle love
with an all consuming wave
of equal rage and love

May 27th

from my lover's embrace
I'm delivered to divine ecstasy
I no longer fear the encroaching evil
in these delicate arms
holding me tightly
so I may hear this heart beat
and be soothed by its sound

life has found a new meaning
a new sound
in these delicate arms

my prayers have been answered
and I have been delivered from harm
the hounds called off
and the deer will return in time
thanks to my lover's delicate arms

May 28th

I crave the endless days
free from fluorescent rays
glaring down upon me
so bright I can barely see

I crave the unending freedom
to roam in nature's kingdom
live amongst her once more
as I once did before
the wrath of men
took me from the glen
and tossed me away
painting the world gray

May 29

I've ventured into evil's haze
walked through it and stayed true
even in the crossfire of its cruel gaze
knowing I had to to see you
the one who rid me of the shackles

the one who put them on and made a show
of taking them off
the one who did this to me

the one who called the hounds
and scared off the deer

oh dear God
my savior is nothing but a farce
a fake, manipulative façade

they drag me back to the shore
threatening to throw me in
acting as if backing out last second
is an act of heroism

May 30

my mind races
finding thousands of meanings
to try and explain their actions
why would they pretend to help
with the suffering they created?

how can they call the hounds
tear me from nature
and still look me in the eyes?

how does meeting my gaze
and telling me how much I'm loved
not make guilt overflow
in their barren heart?

I will love them
until I see the hounds' collars
hanging over my head as they feast
I will love them
until I see my lover's number
on the back of their tags

May 31

howls resound all around me
soon bared teeth are all I will see
I feel them closing in
ready to end my life of sin
I run but they run faster
delivering me to the hereafter

my legs give out
and to the sky I shout
that I no longer fear the hounds
I no longer fear empty sounds
howls carrying nothing
but the fear of nothing
empty threats thrown about
to disguise the way out

I've found the way
to see the light of day
so now I stand tall
unmoving, unfazed in the midst of it all

June 1

I stand unwavering
in the face of my unmaking
facing certain death
with an iron will
I face the bloodthirsty hounds
stand tall in the face of suffering
calling their bluff
for even if their bark matches their bite
I can bear the pain and agony
I can bear searing pain flowing through me
but I can no longer bear regret
I can no longer bear to act as an unmoving bystander
in the face of my own suffering
I will no longer regret
for now I will fight

June 2

your eyes no longer welcome me
for now I see what you see
I see hatred under love's veil
I can see how you expect me to fail
surrender myself to you
return to love's ignorant debut
forgetting the pain you put me through
starting this love anew
free from free will
as you slowly fill
my mind with empty words of affirmation
as you return me to my isolation

free from free will
as my mind turns ill
retreating back in
the threads of my mind wearing thin
as you destroy me
so that you can rebuild me
as a mindless reconstruction
stuck inside the corpse of my destruction

June 3

down this path of realization
I risk it all
love and respect
gone as soon as they appeared
gone as the days of silent suffering
where I was painted in the crimson shades
of agony and despair
desolation and annihilation
but as a phoenix rises from the ashes
I take hold of this divine brush
painting over bleeding red
with vibrant green
returning to nature's truth and freedom
my portrait now sparkling
with shades of gold
as the divine light of realization
filters itself through my mind's web
golden light dappling my glowing image

June 4

I find myself stuck between
hello and goodbye
who will I turn into
in your absence?
will I return
to who I once was?
or have you changed me
beyond return
delivered me to my own event horizon

as I claw my way out of your influence
I feel change wash over me
its tide pulling me out to sea

who will I be
when I've rid myself of you
for I've left bruised
but not yet scarred

but did I leave soon enough
to escape annihilation?

June 5

tumbling towards the ground
I fall from our apple tree
bearing rotten fruit
without bloom
rot without life

I fall towards the ground
bruised and battered
rolling under your boot
I lay here helpless
devoid of hope

too alive to stay here
yet
too dead to move

stuck in limbo
between action and acceptance

June 6

you've broken that which cannot be fixed
damning me to life without bloom
taking the buds of my future
and destroying them
picking off the petals
of flowers that have never known bloom
they've never known life
yet they now lay strewn about your feet
lifeless

for the buds that remain
I will sacrifice all I have
all I am
to save that which isn't beyond saving

but still
I know I'll die trying
to save that which is beyond saving
– us

June 7

what will I say to you tonight
as we lie together beneath the starry night
for the love has not yet left my eyes
but I feel it as it dies
I'm running out of things to say to you
before I do what I know I have to
before I leave you here
before I'm done with you, my dear
please let this night be our last
for I don't know how much longer I can last
living and breathing a lie
gradually working up to goodbye
knowing that that hello
will never follow

June 8

I still feel the red hot sting of love
piercing my heart
I still remember the first time
I looked into your eyes
and saw my reflection
smiling back at me

I will never forget you
and forgetting would never be enough
to cleanse myself of your memory

you grow up my spine like ivy
marring ivory construction
though I viciously try to tear you out
you've left scars
gashes deep in my bone
your memory hides there
and I'm scared

what will happen
when it lays itself bare

June 9

I found the war in your eyes
hiding in it my demise
I see the end and the beginning
I see your patience thinning
I've found you
the one that is true
that which lies under the facade
I now see beyond
the lies of love and eternity
now faced with pools of uncertainty
the eyes of a man
that no longer can
face the world and be seen
knowing that you will never be clean
never free from pain and sorrow
forever unable to face tomorrow
for my destruction was a double edged sword
within me your destiny was stored
but war has freed it from its cage
opening the gates of rage

June 10

I plead to the heavens
for divine guidance
how do I break the chains
shackled to my ankles
how do I cut the threads
tying our souls together
how do I escape
that which I was never meant to?

I pray to the stars
for celestial guidance
but they can't be bothered
to answer a lowly mortal
for they are the beginning and the end
the true almighty

I feel them stare back at me
with cold indifference
I reach out
praying to join them
in motionless eternity

June 11

when will this end?
when will my prayers
finally be answered

I've prayed to the world
prayed to the stars
prayed to all that exists
and yet
nothing.

they remain unheard
and unanswered
I remain alone and unheard
as I drown
in a sea of my own agony

if the divine refuse me
I will become the divine
I will reign above them
and remain unmoved
by their pleads for salvation

June 12

this war drives me mad
running me towards the cliff
into the rushing river
that threatens to tear me
from myself
tearing skin from skin
soul from soul
reducing me to a doll
a puppet
for their desires

once more I pray
pray for salvation
but now
it's reduced to an empty gesture
for I know
no answer awaits me
the only answer
lies within me
I will become the answer
– my own savior

June 13

I bare my teeth
not out of joy
but of anger
a threat veiled as love
one day I'll tear you apart
viciously maul you
in order to put an end
to my suffering

I refuse you eternity
I will seek you out
in every life
every dream
every reality
and I will kill you

I refuse you eternity
as you refuse me my unmarred future
I am forever tied to you
eternally craving
the end of eternity

June 14

I run with the hounds
they lead me along a path
that I can never return from

I can feel myself changing
crossing the point of no return
yet still I return
I return to nature
denouncing civilization
I emerge as the incarnation
of nature's wrath
her unending fury

I will tear you apart
as the hounds threatened
to do to me
but for you there is no escape
no miracle will save man
from nature's vengeance

June 15

take me back
to hollow promises
and delusional faith
so that I may stop
that which comes after

let me tear you apart
before you destroy me
let me devour
that which turned me
from man to beast

nature is unforgiving
yet now
I feel that which she cannot
– remorse
fear
regret
regret for that which has not yet happened

let me tear you apart before I tear myself apart

June 16

with steady aim
I bring myself towards your neck
baring my teeth
pressing bone against soft flesh
I feel your heart steadily beating
and all I want
all I'll ever want
is to stop it

in every life
this will be my one wish
my one goal;
destroying you

I pray my memory will cling to your soul
grow on it like ivy
marring it as I've been marred
as the beautiful wall
where I first saw ivy
reflected in your eyes

June 17

how dare you
look at me with such love
pretending to care
about your victim
loving me by day
and killing me by night

yet

I stand here
adoring you
as I always have

silent tears stream down my face

I'll miss you

I'll still love you

no matter what
I'll always long to be yours

June 18

as my hand wraps itself
around your neck
I am pulled between two paths
It takes every ounce of my being
to refrain from choking you to death
killing you as you lay bare
under me in my bed

It takes every ounce of my being
to keep myself from leaving you

I no longer know what I want
or who I am

what did you do to me?

when will I free myself
from the prison of duality
and unending contradiction

June 19

I collapse into your arms
sobbing into you
you hold me
embrace me
without question

you'll never know why
but I will

I'll always know

how I planned to kill
my beloved

June 20

love blooms
within my skull
filling me with ignorant warmth
your memory wraps itself
around my heart

I wish for nothing more
than for it to stay there
as long as I live
for life without you
will never be worth living

June 21

the petals of blossoming love
have fully opened
within my mind
with leaves basking
in the glorious light
of our love

my spine has fused
with its stalk
bone turned to sturdy vine

I've given myself to you
eternally

June 22

I will follow you
across hell's burning sands
and into the abyss
I will stay by your side
until we return to nothingness

I will be by your side
until the endless cycle
meets its end

June 23

flesh is torn
from my charred soles
as we venture
across blackened sand
into the inferno

you stand before me
still as stone
– stoic
yet I see the cracks
and the lava
slowly breaking you
tearing you apart

though I burn
my ashes return
fire spreading my soul
for the forest may burn
but it will never die
as long as the wind
can spread its seeds

June 24

the wind
spreads the seeds
of my annihilation
your breath
delivered it to me

this seed
it controls me
I long to tear it
from my mind
but I fear
I'll escape my skull
my soul
leaking through the gashes
you left in me

June 25

I lay here still
stuck in the overgrowth
of my mind
wound up in vines
that threaten to drag me
back to the walls
where ivy grows wild
destroying
that which it clings to

if I were to die
destroy myself
what would you cling to?

June 26

as the stars
knowingly gaze upon me
bathing me in their faint light
anger wells in my heart
observing me with cold indifference
they watch me pray to them
listen to me beg
yet
they do nothing

I will destroy them
leaving annihilation in my wake
eternally waging war
against all
who stand against me

June 27

I will destroy you
tear you apart
piece by piece
as the wolves
tear into
innocent deer

you are my wolf
and yet
you are the hunted
I watch you as you watch me
plotting your murder
as you plot mine

but the wolves were made for bloodshed
they find comfort in the routine
letting their guard down
around the innocent

egotistical comfort
will be your downfall

June 28

I howl at the moon
running alongside
the hounds
though my skull is adorned
with a crown of bone
they've welcomed me
into their pack
for we share the same goal;
annihilation of the wicked
of those that seek our destruction

through them I've learned
the art of the hunt
and the delicate act
of closing the distance
between predator and prey
regardless of which
is hunting the other

June 29

pain and agony
light up my mind
as I tear myself apart
searching for you
hunting down
the remnants of your memory
lodged in my spine

I lead myself to the edge
of life and death
as I tear you out
of my life
of my heart
thorns hook into bleeding flesh
taking pieces of me
with you

even as I tear you out of me
dead and lifeless
you still try
to take me down with you

June 30

from deep gashes
I bleed
onto concrete floors
and broken glass

I'm free
yet
I can't move
I lay here motionless
unable even to bite
at your neck as you hold me
pushing me into your chest

I feel your mocking heartbeat
as you cry into me
begging me
to get help
to seek treatment

the only treatment I'll ever need
is your death

July 1

I sit here enveloped in warmth
surrounded by empty gestures
of love and adoration
why must you sit there
looking at me
with such warmth in your eyes?

why must your eyes hold such warmth
only after their coldness
froze my heart
and brought me to the verge
of annihilation
by my own
shaking hands

July 2

I sit here trapped
in your prison of empty promises
wrapped in false affections
you play the part of a lover
in your eyes I find nothing
but overwhelming love and adoration
yet I feel hatred
stirring beneath the surface
indignation
at my condition
and the position you find yourself in

driven near death
I've removed your seed
mind altering parasite
I can't tell
if you've figured me out
or you still think

I'm in love with you

July 3

the wounds close
the bleeding stops
but the mind
is forever altered
the gashes across my back
are forever engraved
in my mind
forever etched
into my soul

I'll never forget
the removal of ivy
from its desperate host

I'll never forget
how the garlic mustard
clung to my skull
as I pulled it from my brain
grey matter
stuck to its roots

July 4

colorful explosions
full my eyes and ears
as I rest in your arms
your love is violence
an eternal war of loveless rage
yet as I doze off in your arms
I feel nothing but safe

I will forever mourn the person
you could've been
and how our love
could've been
if we had the chance
to do it all again
love each other
when we're finally ready
for that love

we could've been great
if only we loved
at a different time

July 5

I wish we could heal these wounds
heal that which has ruined us
but these scars run too deep
no matter how hard I try
I'll never be able to see you
without the shadows of your past
dancing across your eyes

please darling
find me again
years from now
let us love
when we're ready for love

July 6

when we're better people
better lovers
I'll send for you
whisper your name through the ether
bring us back together
when our scars have faded
and the wounds are no longer fresh

I'll forever mourn
what could've been
if we met at our best
instead of our worst
if we met as fully formed people
instead of emerging adults

July 7

my body has been taken from me
along with my will
I pleaded
I begged and pleaded
anything else
let us bond
without carnal desire

your heart holds the coldness
of the stars
I know my pleas reached you
for you fought against them
refusing them
forcing me
forcing us

this love was doomed from the start
but now I need you more than ever
to try and make this feel okay
so I don't look at you
and see a monster

July 8

meet not my gaze
but see into my heart
see how you've marred it
look into the gashes
left behind
by bitter garlic mustard
watch as the white flowers
still circulate through my body

the ivy was the least of it
oh dear god the ivy was the best of it
now you've left me only with
bitter garlic mustard
clinging to my beating heart

I sit here wondering
what else I missed
do thorns grow within
that I'm yet to find

July 9

I beg for you to stay
and for you to go
I will never be free
with you
yet I can never live freely
in your absence
you've destroyed me
forced me to rely only on you
for all I do
and all I feel

my life is forever
tied to yours
and I'd do anything
to cut the threads
even if it means
I die in the process

I no longer fear death
for this life is no longer living

July 10

I desperately search for a way
to save me and keep you away
I plead for needle and thread
so I can stay away from bed
away from you
and that which you beg to do
to me as I lay here still
giving myself up to your will
I've lost the will to fight
for that which I know is right
so now I hold this needle tight
to keep you away for tonight

white thread turns crimson
as I free myself from the prison
of carnal desire
as my flesh is set on fire
and my soul is released

July 11

from fire I was born
and to fire I return
from the still burning embers
of the forest
I've been reborn
as revenge incarnate
a deer that has risen from the ashes
now hungry for flesh

the sun is setting
on your life's horizon
while you chase after
the last, dying rays of light
I stay behind
rising the moon
and pushing down
the sun

July 12

I hold the embers in my heart
left in the ruins of the forest
you burned it down
and smoked me out
without rhyme nor reason
cruelty for the sake of it
destroying all that I had
all that I ever knew

I will use this body as kindle
to light the pyre of revenge
as the embers in my heart
grow ever hotter
in the wake
of your end

July 13

in your absence I've been freed
free to roam and wander
the endless woods
with hounds at my heels
that no longer strike out against me
they feel the embers
burning inside
see smoke leave my mouth
with every word
this murderous fervor is infectious
spreading on the backs
of the hounds' calls

with each howl
I feel the forest rise with me
towards the annihilation
of man

July 14

burning heat
flows in my veins
disintegrating
the last of you
and your power
over me

you've become
mere ash
dust on the floor
you'll never rise
from where you've fallen

July 15

the hounds call for you
lure you into the forest
where the trees sway
in the raging wind
the deer have grown fangs
to drag you down
into your shallow grave
beneath the apple tree
that has never known bloom

July 16

when will no be enough
to keep you away

I've begged and pleaded
for you to go
yet you stay
you stay and you use me

I've tried all I can
to keep the hounds at bay
I never wanted it
to come down to this
but now
I feel no remorse
for what I know comes next

because no
didn't keep you away
and you continued on
conquering my body
as I lay bare and broken

July 17

jaws snap
teeth against teeth
dazzling white
under the dark sky

no star shines as bright
as the fire of desire
I hold in my burning heart
I've forgotten for whom it burns
or for what it burns
but I know
it will be the death of me
desire has become obsession
and obsession borders mania

I pray the wind
will extinguish my fire
for now I am lucid
aware of what comes next
and all I want
is to return to silence and sanity

July 18

this brief return of my wits
has left me shaken
scared of what comes next
when I return to obsession

I feel myself
falling back into the void
where reason will no longer reach me

despite my fear
I know that this must happen
I must return to the all consuming void
of obsessive destruction
I have to destroy
the one who destroyed me
even if it means
I'm destroyed in the process

July 19

I sit under our tree
as the sky tears itself apart
brilliant strikes of lightning
break through the cracks
as rain pours down
flooding the world
it once overlooked
in the midst of the heavens madness
I send a silent prayer
hoping it seeps through
the cracks

please
strike me as I sit here
beneath our tree
may I burn and char
with our dying love

July 20

I feel your heart shifting
the embers stirred and reborn
erupting in flame
as they're given new life
your hands burn with emotion
scouring my body
searching every last piece
as if burning it into memory

from the ashes of my demise
you've found new life
snuffing me out
to find your own flame

July 21

I burned far too bright
losing my spark along the way
losing sight of what is right
of what I saw in you that day
the love burning in your heart
and the flame in your eyes
memory threatens to tear me apart
as my heart slowly dies

July 22

the stars envy
my burning heart
for it is charred and barren
yet still aflame
burning without fuel
outshining every star across the sky
persisting on hate
divine vengeance
pushes me forward
fueling my every move
as I prepare for the celestial war
of nature and man
waiting to see
which one the tide will claim

July 23

I urge you to embrace flight
soar as the birds
leap from this stone
and free yourself
from man made suffering
you claim to not know flight
yet you've never tried

I urge you to embrace flight
join me as we soar
above the world
as the rulers of the sky

I urge you to embrace flight
as I sharpen my talons
against the cliff's stone
for though you're flightless
a wingless mouse
I swear I'll catch you
for I'm starving
and cannot risk letting you go

July 24

scorching sun
leaves me undone
lain out on the grass
praying for this to pass
for the sun to set
on what we started when we met
I've waited for too long
knowing this was wrong
I pray to end this
before the abyss
returns to me
and forces me to be
mindlessly destructive
my heart eruptive
as lava flows through me
for I know not another way to be free

the blazing sun has shed light
on what I know is right
– I must kill to be free

July 25

I feel the threads unravel
as I release mental tension
I allow myself to return
to the hounds and deer
sharpening my wit
against shining bone
my path to salvation
illuminated by a growing moon
the light of madness
overtaking rational darkness
I follow it like a moth to flame
burning myself out
as I chase that which consumes me
body and soul

July 26

leave me in the dark
with only fate
to keep me company
let that which ails me
consume me as I consume myself
and I'll embrace my descent into madness
as I once embraced you

I pray you'll find this diary
for through prose and poetry
I need you to read my thoughts
watch me slowly dying
at the hands of your actions
willingly fanning the flames
of your destruction

you did this
when you raped me
and made my mind up for me
sending me down the path
of mutual destruction

July 27

find me under our tree
buried beneath
I wait for you here
wait for you to follow your heart
to that which you know you can't be without
I know you need me
but I never needed you
I was the best you'll ever get
and you the worst I'll ever know

I'll drag you down here with me
buried under the infernal grudge
of cruel love

you've broken my heart beyond breaking
gone beyond failed love and further down
down into my soul
but you struck wrong
hitting sanity and not psyche
chaining yourself to death
as I've never felt more free

July 28

I burn brighter than ever
seething with rage
in the darkness of my room
embracing shadows
I once fled from
my eyes see naught
yet have never seen more
I've filed my once harmless teeth
to flesh ripping daggers
breaking my skin
to find a taste for blood
so I may seek it out
and not recoil at the taste
for you are a feast
I'd be damned to leave

July 29

I watch the moon grow
nearly ready
to illuminate my mind
shine in through my eyes
show me the way
to annihilation and salvation
I beg for you to find me now
as I lie in wait
preparing to sink my fangs
into your neck
draining you
watching you bleed on the floor
would be a dream come true
I fear I can't wait
for the moon to fill

I need you now
please baby
I miss you

July 30

fire has consumed me
I sit here ablaze
embracing flame and ferocity
watching skin melt
and hair char
bone revealed
as I fall out of myself
the brain separate from the body
soul no longer knowing flesh
free from physical constraints
free to roam the ether
and sow the seeds
of self destruction
and eternal devotion
in your sleepless dreams

July 31

the moon beckons me
calls me into its all knowing light
washing over me
in waves of wisdom
giving me tastes of freedom
so that I may never forget
the joy of annihilation
and my mission
of eliminating man
so that my heart may once more bloom
in secluded ecstasy
so that sea and nature
may once more join hand and hand
no longer forced to be at odds
with the others
the stars will regain their warmth
as balance returns to nature's kingdom
in the absence of man
as they are forced
into a perpetual cycle

of self destruction and eternal devotion

for that which they cannot have

the moon will watch over all

as nature plants the seeds

of man's annihilation

watching them laugh

at their presumed freedom

as we wait patiently

for roots to grow

and take over

the prospect of what could've been

blooming as an eternal obsession

only after

it is beyond the point of return

August 1

the final clash
of man and nature
has left the earth stained
as crimson blood
flows through its streams
dying even the sea red
as the life of man
has been ended
by my snapping jaws
for as thunder follows lightning
bite has followed bark
tearing flesh from flesh
breaking all in my path
of blind destruction

bones bend and break
as I push through
to man's beating heart
infecting it with longing
as the connection is severed

between us
I watch you now
lifeless and broken beyond recognition
as the hounds rush forward
devouring your memory
nearly choking on vomit
as they spill their stomachs
in the hole
where I once kept your memory
bile rises in my throat
as I see through love's delusion

deer hurry forth
dragging you away
to the tree we once shared
the earth caving in
as the sky breaks apart
rain pouring down
extinguishing my heart's flame
as roots pull you down
into the shallow grave you dug
never knowing it would become yours

August 2

from my chest pours crimson
aching from a wound
I never thought I'd have
my heart has been ripped from me
gone without a trace
and I fear the worst
that I left it with yours
our veins entwined
mine pulled from my chest
as I pulled out yours
buried beneath our tree
soaking the soil and roots
with the cold blood
of a victor's defeat

August 3

cold hearts no longer beat
without flame a candle cannot burn
my body has run out of steam
revenge no longer fuels me
still and cold
unmoving and unliving
victory has taken all
salvation bringing destruction

my heart no longer beats
without your love's warmth

August 4

I miss you
as blades miss skin
begging for sweet slaughter
and for crimson waves
to crash upon the ground
let my internal sea
spill out
just as all rivers connect to the sea
all my love will always connect to you
I will find a piece of you in every lover
and in all the world's beauty

I wish I knew you
when you had shed the skin
of ruinous action
emerging from the chrysalis
of adolescent ego

August 5

find me
when you're better
when you're kind
when pain softens your heart
in the places you need it
let the world wear on you
until you understand what you left behind
find me then
I'll take you
forgive our past
and embrace our future

August 6

I will never forgive you
and I will never forget you
I will remember you
in pain and in passion
in shades of desire and devastation
through the prism of all emotion
your memory shines through
flooding my mind
with bittersweet murder
as you send me into
a spiral of self annihilation
happy as a clam
at the thought of what we could've been
and in fleeting moments
how you were

August 7

the sea weeps with me
mourning what could've been
churning waves
turned to quiet tides
as she gives me the strength
to return to nature
I cry into her
begging for forgiveness
for now I know her violence
was never violent
she was powerful formidable
a goddess knowing her worth
and ruling over that which was hers
with absolute authority

as I return to nature
I invite the sea to join me
for I wish to capture her essence
and carry it within my soul

August 8

my tears run to the stars
begging them to return me
to ignorant love
back to when my mind
was not my own
controlled by the parasitic narrative
of violent love

I miss you like an addict
knowing you destroyed my brain
yet willing to do anything
to leave this uncertainty behind me
and return to the midst of love's warmth

August 9

beneath the tree
of dying love
rosettes turn to rot
wilting and falling
before even our tree
sheds its leaves
delicate white flowers
will never again bloom
for my buried heart
seeps hatred into the soil
more potent than any poison

trembling in the breeze
leaves fall
as tears hit the ground
falling like the rain
on the night of broken skies
and shattered hearts

August 10

your ghost
floats above
hiding in clouds
following the breeze
back to a time
where love was loving
and romance was not yet empty
with the ash of love's pyre
following suit
but the wind refuses me
parting in the face
of my charred heart
I beg to join
return to life before death
but I never will

I trek on
down my own path
of love after the pyre
and I feel the sunlight
readying my heart for spring

August 11

I breath in
and out
my breathe
no longer ablaze
no longer burning my throat
with the fire of hate
I stand here reborn
for I died when I left you
died and left in a grave of agony
but I clawed my way out
the dirt still under my nails
death destroyed me
and I get to rebuild myself
turn myself into someone better
stronger and wiser
and for that I thank you

I will always thank you
for my annihilation
and letting me leave you

August 12

I miss the scorching agony
of fire lacing my every word
I miss when tears shook me
drowning me in emotion
when tears ran black
burning my eyes
I found solace in the routine
of intense love and immediate heart break
I was in love with pain
you just were the one to give it to me
I pray for your return
for the return of unending agony
I would do anything
for you to kill me again

August 13

metal knives
don't cut as deep
as the knife hidden
in your every word
please come back to me
agony kept me sane
it kept me alive
searing pain
kept me inspired
without you what will I write?
this diary is already in pieces
poetry no longer has its ring
becoming just pretentious prose

I pray for your return
my agonizing muse

August 14

the lost can be found
and the found can be lost
but I fear I am neither
not lost nor found
I am damned to purgatory
I do my best to be found
but I will always be lost
without you
why did I ever leave you
you were the glue keeping
my broken parts together
though they were shattered by your hand
you put them back together again
you put me together
to break me apart again
but at least I was together
I don't know how to put myself back together
without you I'm damned to be broken
pieces fall off of me
I pick them up and try to put them back
but without you nothing sticks

August 15

summer's sun
blazes above the horizon
and as she paints the sky
in crimson and scarlett
I weep for us
I still remember you here
beneath our tree
with her dying light
painting your face
in crimson beauty

I hate that I miss you
for I know you ruined me
and that you were the death of me
I miss the familiarity
of you by my side
for without you
I have no one

August 16

you killed me
mind and soul
rape cuts deeper
than anything else
you ever could've done
I weep for you
for I know you know what you did
and still you allow yourself life
how can you live on so easily
knowing you damned me
to a life of shame and misery

August 17

I find your face
in every shadow
you haunt me
your memory
refusing to let go of me
please let me go
let me live
as one unburdened
by the unbreakable chains
of rape and coercion
that you've shackled me to

August 18

divine freedom
shines through the trees
as nature welcomes me back
the forest rising in song
as I make my return
back to sunny days
and greener grass
the air hits my lungs
crisp and clear
for the first time since you
I'm free to breath without choking
the threads between us
have been burned by the sun
as she frees me
from that which you forced upon me

healing is a process
but with every step I take
into nature's beautiful kingdom
wounds begin to close
and scars begin to fade

August 19

I become one with the trees
my skin merging with bark
I gain their infinite wisdom
as I tap into roots
deeper than any human knowledge
the Earth is part of me
and she is all I am
I am the raging seas
and the tranquil forest
I have the power to shape her
she has shown herself to me
vulnerable and true

before me lay two paths
both lead to destruction
I know not which is right
should I return to the hunting hounds
or return my body to dirt

annihilation awaits me at the end of each

August 20

I see you through the ether
rage no longer consumes me
and love no longer blinds me
I see you as what you are
a disgusting mess
a stain on society
vermin that needs to be exterminated
you don't deserve life
you deserve nothing more than death
complete and total death
first the mind and then the soul
dead as your body lives on
dying only after
everyone around you goes first

I will kill you
for it is my duty
to set the example for all others
to destroy those who destroy others
even if society deems me a villain
I know it must be done and it must be done by me

August 21

the deer have lost their fangs
and the hounds their bite
left only with dull hooves
and empty howls
but we will find you
hidden beneath the cloak of innocence
for our goal has shifted
the end delayed
death alone no longer satisfies
the cravings of the damned

we will deliver hell to your doorstep
in the name of our collective suffering
hell itself will pale in comparison
to that which we will unleash
onto those which have preyed upon us
and taken our bodies hostage

August 22

I watch you dare to live
in the face of what you've done
freely indulging
in that which life has to offer
while I've been damned
to a life of delivering justice
I never asked for this
I never wanted to have my life
taken from me
but now that it's gone
it will never come back
and so I gather the hounds
train them on your scent
and dare to take matters into my own hands
as I devise my plan
to shine light on your crime
and let those you hold close
see the shadow of your actions
that you've so desperately tried to hide

August 23

do the hounds know what's right
do they think before they attack
or do they just follow orders
I no longer know which path is right
for annihilation can be avoided
I ask the trees what to do
and instantly they go still
rustling leaves falling silent
as I'm left with nothing
but the sound of my own beating heart

I pray for your death
but I owe myself life
and dedicating myself to your death
is nothing more
than dedicating myself to you

nails pierce through skin
uncovering rivers of flowing crimson
as the sea pours from my eyes
I want nothing more than to be rid of you

August 24

I can no longer bear
the sound of this life unfair
left with nothing but the sound
of my heart buried in the ground
beating for the sake of it
refusing to admit
that life has lost its ring
at the hand of love's sting
that which I've always sought
and I once thought I caught
slipping through my trembling fingers
as your memory lingers
in the front of my brain
driving me insane
I pray for release
for this feeling to cease
– for me to finally be free

August 25

show me the path to freedom
to escape the world from which I come
leave behind my sorrow and pain
let my suffering be not in vain
my life needs a reason
but I fear my heart's treason
left it behind; unreturnable
though my scars are irreversible
my heart reaches through the soil
I feel my body recoil
from the rotting remains
of the one who bound me to these chains
of regret and eternal shame
that forced me into self blame
eternally bound
to the still bleeding ground

August 26

let the clouds
fall from the sky
and onto you
let them obscure you
so I never see you again
for your face is haunting
peering out at me
from every shadow
threatening to bring me back
to the days of loveless torture
it drives me closer to the edge
everytime I see it

I want nothing more
than to be rid of you
though our hearts belong to the same soil
we will never belong to another again
you will never bind me back to the shackles
of dying to be loved

August 27

sea water pours
from my empty chest
pushing its way
through my ribcage
breaking bones
and punching through flesh
as the pressure builds
begging for escape

August 28

salt water flows through me
as the sea takes my heart
to her rocky shores
thorns dig into my skin
as vines pull me back
to the forest
begging for me to return
to nature and her healing light
but I fear I'm far too damaged
to be whole again
so I give myself to the sea
let her sting my open wounds
as salt tortures me how I was tortured before
letting pain fuel my fire
as I give myself up to desire

August 29

blood spills from my open chest
though I've tried my best
to halt my descent
into perpetual self torment
all roads lead here
into that which I fear
a life where I keep my heart exposed
in an open wound that will never be closed
and the salty air stings my heart
as I watch the sea part
welcoming me along the path
to an all consuming wrath
where the water will always burn
and I can never return
to love and light
because for me, this is right

I'm willing to accept my fate
as one made for hate

August 30

my bloods flows with the current
and rises with the waves
dying the ocean red
with my fading life
the cold holds me
like its child
but we both know
I don't belong
in this sea of despair
life has taken me
from love and light
driven me into a corner
and now like a frightened animal
I speak only with claws and teeth
destroying them before they can find me
taking the ocean's violence into my open heart
for I refuse to be taken for a fool again
I will bite and scratch until the end

September 1

through the water's haze
I see flowing green
dancing in the current
salt flows from my eyes
disappearing in the water
though my heart has now embraced
the stinging pain of destiny's threads
as they're sewed into it with every beat
I will never forget
my days spent
under dazzling rays
dappling the ground beneath me
as they filter through the trees
that await my return
to painless freedom

September 2

ghosts of health and prosperity
haunt me as they pass
riding on the backs of turtles
sheer sheets of green algae
remind me of days long gone
that I may never return to
for I have forged chains
of salt and sand
that bind me to the ocean's floor
keeping me from the surface
where I can breathe the air
and follow the winds
back home
where my heart lays buried
in my tree's roots

September 3

blood flows in the current
and I wonder where it goes
does it long for the tree
as I do?
or did it lose emotion
once it left me
adapting to the sea's cold nature
leaving emotion to those that can afford it
to those left dry

September 4

let me breathe in
wet smoke
intoxicating fumes
that drown themselves
in sorrow

beautiful flower
laced with pain
this dazzling flame
threatens to dry me
should I let the momentary lucidity
it whispers in my ear
infiltrate my mind
and revitalize me
where garlic mustard
laid me bare
and pumped me full of poison

September 5

salt crystals shine in dying light
growing upon exposed bone
eating through my fading plight
my body slowly sinks alone
through the freezing cold
of water too scared to freeze

September 6

I lost myself
in my reflection again
retracing my every line
until they begin to entwine
growing a mind of their own
swimming through glass like water
they venture alone
leaving me behind
as they take on their own shape
I pray they'll be safe
on their adventures through a sea of glass
as they leave me blank
left to rot
without a face

September 7

the mirror's cracks have begun to flow
as my hand gives it the freedom it craves
to flow as the magnificent sea
breaking free of its stagnancy
white crests have already formed
heading waves that have not yet surfaced
I already feel the salt
as the sea clings to my hand
begging to join the ebb and flow
of my weakening pulse
glass currents pull my crimson tide
far out to sea

September 8

fire licks flame
forcing the sand
to glow as it flows
red as the dying sun
liquid as the sea
it comes back to me
back to the shores
it was stolen from
glass loses its heart
finding shelter in my own
as crimson tide
and salty sweat
reminds it of home

September 9

I watch the sea
break free of stagnancy
stalk the moon
and I watch it swoon
as moonlight washes over
the waves she extends to her
she chases her with no end
praying love is around the bend
but nothing waits there
though she's laid her heart bare
her obsession will only end
as they forcibly descend
into another
as fate's strings tangle together

September 10

white shores of chalk
bodies lay cold in shock
the sirens call
comes for all
vessels large and small
will eventually fall
crumbling under the weight
of egos far too great
for creatures of the land
that think they're more than sand
the sea will claim all
when men crumble and fall

September 11

cut your ties
to manmade lies
let go the anchor
that binds you to her
sever that which connects
you to your regrets

let her free
to sink into the sea
for salty tears cannot burn
when there's nothing left to yearn

September 12

you have taken it all
survived the rise and fall
but what did you leave behind
within my infected mind
I still see streaks of green
appear and disappear between
moments of calm reflection
where I mourn your affection
for I know I was a fool to stay
as I long as I did until that day
but you still cross my mind from time to time
and I mourn that which could have been mine
though you were never as you seemed
I always prayed you'd be redeemed
you showed me nothing but hate
but I still mourn the idea of you, once great

September 13

the sea has washed away
the fog that's haunted me since that day
when trust was broken
and hatred left unspoken
when you saw me bare
marred me without care
I will forever be haunted by you
no matter what I do

you've forced your way into my body and mind
and I've been forced to leave myself behind

this clarity is fleeting, I know
but I promise to find you no matter where you go

I will find you and kill you once more
I dream of nothing but you and gore

September 14

wash me out
separate me from sin
without a doubt
this is the best state I've been in
since my world collapsed around me
as fireflies fled from July
I've given myself to the sea
within her I thought I'd die
but I've emerged upon chalky shores
shed my mortal fear and worry
left with nothing but sores
and celestial fury

September 15

salt dries
on a body that forgot the sun
new light shines in its eyes
internal wars are done
gone from nature to man
to the bottom of the sea
I return to where I began
to where I am supposed to be
the body strides on
while the mind's left reeling
something feels wrong
I don't understand this feeling
am I finally free
from the torment of man
can I finally be
as I am?

September 16

sand clings to palms still moist
as I stand unmoving on unknown shores
salt crystals hang from my hair
and the sun bakes me from dawn to dusk
legs stride confidently on
as the mind is left in the water
salt replacing invasive weeds
the bitter smell of crushed garlic mustard
still clings to my nose
but it no longer clings to my mind
this sudden clarity is what shakes me
I can no longer think
without my familiar fog
clouding my thoughts

I cry tears of sweat freedom
as I make my way down chalky shores

I praise the sea
for saving me

September 17

revenge is left
but an empty threat
as I adjust to newfound heft
no longer suspended in the wet
embrace of spiritual cleansing
I have found new meaning
as I begin ascending
leaving behind days left screaming
for an experience
that was never worth the agony

September 18

lungs freely breathing
with the weight taken away
I can finally start returning
to where I was led astray
without the pain it brought me
I return with nothing but joy
as I am refreshed by time in the sea
free to finally enjoy
life without burden

September 19

though I walk alone
I'm not afraid of the unknown
I alone am enough
my heart was a fire you couldn't snuff
and now it burns beautifully
upon the pyre I made from thee
your memory turns to ash
blown away in a flash
as the salty wind propels me
back to where I ought to be

September 20

I bid farewell to salty seas
and weightless tranquility
days spent drowning
in myself and my misery

I bid you farewell
salty tears trace my cheeks
and I pray to one day return
to show you what I made of my life
the life you've freed me to live

waves crash and tears fall
on chalky shores I grew to love
I swear
I won't let goodbye be eternal

September 21

I stall for a moment
as grass meets sand
I've grown dependent
on what comes before land
I've left behind my tears
but I still must face my fears

careful, I tread on green grasses
with breath shaking
each step slow as molasses
as I feel my heart breaking
but I still press onward
pushing my life forward

I silently beg of thee
to remember me
the way I'll remember you

September 22

butterflies swarm
while gales warm
clothes still drying
I feel like I'm flying
as I leap and bound
dancing around
meadows once forgotten
beneath clouds of cotton

I've missed simple freedoms like this
dancing among flowers in pure bliss

September 23

brilliant light
shines through
warming my skin
and heart buried beneath
teeth reflect back at her
as I smile with body and soul
facing the sun
on a day she'll never die

September 24

seas of green
wash over rolling hills
painting a scene
where nature and sea collide
she's found me
though the shore separates us
our souls now entwined
she follows me on my journey
back to days where sorrow
hadn't yet found me

I smile at her as I continue on
and for a second
I hear waves crashing

September 25

my heart will never fall
behind the horizon
I am a sun that will never set
dawn without dusk
in time I will fall
but I will fight
against the dying light
with tooth and nail
as the hounds fought me
and I fought betrayal
my heart glows
pushing through skin

I am a being greater
than I've ever been

September 26

life's winding path
has led me down hills and valleys
paved with love and wrath
into dark alleys
without hope for light
at the end of the tunnel
teaching me how to bite
as I'm buried in the rubble
of hopes lost and gone
and bridges burned
with me still on
from it I've learned
– learned how to bite
but I still don't know
when the time is right
so I stand motionless like a doe
blinded by headlights on the freeway
paralyzed by fear
not knowing when to fight or run away

September 27

as I return to familiar roads
facing familiar faces
I bare my teeth
from my time under crushing waves
I saw cruelty run rampant
no place on Earth is safe
friend and foe have become one

I thought I was ready
to live amongst deer again
but I've become the hounds
chasing them down

deer become hounds
prey becomes predator
the hurt hurt

September 28

I sit alone
backing myself into a corner
every motion
every glance
screams danger
all I see are deer
but I can't overcome my fear
of snapping jaws
tearing me apart
undressing me
and taking the little hope I've found

I thought I was ready to live again

September 29

shadows taunt me
on my drunk walk home
stumbling downhill
I see your face
– my death
in every passerby
headlights rush towards us
and I pray they hit us both
I will walk away unscathed
for death can't find me twice
but you will die there
covered in your own blood
choking on your own spit
my only regret
will be not making it hurt more

September 30

bottles scatter
on linoleum floors
but they're not the one to shatter
as my heart seems to have forgotten the shores
to which we fled
and from which we returned
my shirt's stained with red
familiar places have churned
memories I buried to heal
bottled up inside
so I'd never have to feel
that which I left to the tide

next time I'll bury you
in trenches where even light refuses
to explore the dark blue
the same color as my bruises

October 1

in and out
I breathe slow
my heart has no place for doubt
only joy can grow
in my garden of healing
where flowers dot the land
buds bloom revealing
vibrant petals as they expand
growing with the love I shower them in
hyacinths and roses grow together
in my heart free from sin
eternal bloom no matter the weather
no blight will find us here

October 2

with delicate hands
I unwind the roots
of the weeds that entwine
with my flowers
bit by bit
inch by inch
I unravel their vicious hold
freeing my flowers
from their strangling grip

deceiving white flowers
with leaves of jagged spade
are banished from my garden
and sent to burn

October 3

atop the pyre
of thieving weeds
sits the throne of desire
starved of its needs
no longer living within
my mind drained of reason
and filled with sin
burned alive for its treason
I refuse to be blinded
by its influence again

October 4

ash is blown
across the sky
falling upon places once known
before the throne's fall
grey snow descends
upon new blooms
snuffing out the sun
shaking hands brush off
as much as they can
but the garden is buried
weaker flowers culled
for the greater good
the soul has died
to usher in a better life

October 5

death stretches beyond the horizon
painted red by the dying sun
grief has poured itself over the garden
through waterfalls of salt
and rivers of crimson waves
life will bloom again
flowers will grow back
even more gorgeous than before
but first the slate must be wiped clean
healing is a journey
and I pray this is its end
for it closes chapter after chapter
without hope for a conclusion

please
let the sun rise on greener grasses
and may it never set so cruelly again

October 6

survivors plunged into darkness
starved for warmth
kept alive by rivers not yet dry
that have carved their way
through this desolate garden
feeding off pain
has made them grow stronger
doing whatever it takes to survive
preparing themselves for the day
they can gorge themselves
on a new sun

October 7

nuclear winter
has fallen on radioactive bloom
hope a barely burning cinder
narrowly keeping out the gloom
lives half over and over
but never reach death
edging ever closer
never drawing its last breath
barely alive
buried in ash
is it worth it to survive
wishing every breath was your last

October 8

plunged into darkness

my eyes no longer see

in darkness I confess

I don't know who I'm meant to be

nothing is left to distract

my mind from introspection

I've become what I attract

one unworthy of affection

in the dark I see your light

the one you lit inside me

to outshine what is right

so I couldn't see how close I was to being free

I've done my best to snuff you out

but my efforts only fan your flame

all I can do now is wait it out

until I'm free from the person I became

October 9

dark as the ocean
I'm back at square one
an infinite cycle of healing
until your influence has been undone
I draw ever closer
to an unattainable goal
you've consumed my life
my heart and soul
I will never rid myself
of the scars you carved into me
but I can change them
mold them to better fit my needs
turn pain into passion
devastation into inspiration

October 10

I will light my own flame
feeding upon the carcass
of the one I was before
I've died a thousand times
and I'll die a thousand more
with each new chapter
the old will fuel my pyre
it will push me forward
until I burn so bright
I outshine all around me
and all the little flames
I've let people light in me

October 11

I rise from my own ashes
pushing my way
through my own coffin
rising from death
with the sun rising at my back
basking in the light of a new day

I will burn brighter
than ever before
with the past as my fuel
my future will outshine
the new sun

October 12

from inside my heart's cage
my flame grows ever brighter
burning away all my rage
my soul begins to feel lighter
the shackles that once held me
have begun to melt away
in my light I can now see
clearly the light of the next day
my future has left the shadows
and I see it clearer than crystal

October 13

with the weeds gone
life has lost momentum
freed from the agonizing cycle
of life without rest
I sit on the porch
and truly feel the moment
for the first time
since we met beneath the tree
where my heart still clings
to ravenous roots

yours was never truly there
existing only in passing
and you dashed back and forth
to other trees
grown upon beating hearts

my tree is free from you
the garlic mustard long gone
all I can do now is take life slow
and wait to bloom

October 14

I dragged my heart through the mud
after the rains of heartbreak
saturated the soil
blindly following an imaginary path
that promised to lead me
to health and prosperity
there was no end there
only pain
as you engulfed my life
my own healing focused on your end

I thought I found a shortcut to happiness
but I was caught up in
the mudslide of revenge

I found my way out
though mud still dries on my clothes

I'll try to live for myself now
meandering down life's path
slow but steady

October 15

from dawn to dusk
the sun glimmers like rust
shadows ebb and flow
under her golden glow
birds sing for her arrival
fanfare celebrating revival
the promise of a new day
will never go away
but still we rejoice
at the sight of her choice
to rise above us once again
share her beauty even with cruel men
who thrive beneath her
living in spite of her
using her light for their own needs
becoming one with the weeds

October 16

fallen gold
covers the ground
now too brittle to hold
crumbling as soon as it's found
following the wind as dust
free to venture past the tree
dulled the color of rust
as it learns the price to be free
nothing in this life is without cost
no freedom without sacrifice
life in the wind a reminder of what is lost
with no replacement that shall suffice
when the wind tears you from home
and freedom keeps you alone

October 17

time has returned
to clocks that no longer chime
and a mind that has turned
stagnant now that time
is time again
a steady stream
free from the hands of men
who turned it to steam
concentrating the time spent in pain
and evaporating the time spent healing
– but now it rains
and now I know what I'm feeling
a downpour of that which was lost
has returned to wilting flowers
at the cost
of learning how to enjoy new hours

I missed timeless freedom
but life slowed leaves me feeling meaningless

October 18

shadows dance across bare walls
and I feel like I'm behind bars
sitting here remembering these halls
that I ran through praying to the stars
for an end to loveless madness
as tears connected me to the sea
drowning in overwhelming sadness
I forgot that I was me
I was I
I've always been myself
but ever since July
I've put my soul on a shelf
collecting dust
as I rotted in the light
of the sun's dying rust
immortalizing my death as I write

October 19

deer stare me down
from beneath streetlights
venturing into town
no longer scared of fights
between nature and man
prepared to see the earth
now that they finally can
embrace lives of joy and mirth
away from snapping jaws
and everlasting sorrow
returning to life without pause
now that they know they'll see tomorrow

I stare back
into watery eyes
without fear of attack
while we stand beneath star filled skies
a silent treaty has been signed
with a knowing glance
our hearts are once again aligned
as we are locked in this trance

October 20

fate has cut lines through the grass
marking where the deer pass
through paths unseen
marking their constant routine
hooves travel down roads
forged as they erode
the ground below
following trails only they know

as fawn follows doe
I wonder if they know
that there was once grass
covering their beloved pass

was mother once like fawn
or was the path already drawn
when her mother led
her down this path already tread

October 21

brisk winds of fallen leaves
fall from shedding trees
yet the invading green
a devastating sight, unclean
I'll wash and scrub my skin
to resolve me of sin
but my eyes have seen
a river of green
wash away hope and love
forcing me to look above
for a force beyond what I know
to send a blizzard of decimating snow
to destroy this wretched foe
in its place will grow
a forest of flowers and glory
erasing a war dirty and gory
from the minds of those
who woefully chose
to fight on the front lines
and bring back nature, divine

October 22

war has ended
but my life is still upended
I try with all my might
but I'll never forget the night
of the final bloody fight
between wrong and right
I once knew to which side
I fought til I nearly died
but now as your memory
haunts me as a tainted reverie
was it ever worth it
to take my arms and slit
let crimson tides flow
while I'll know
you weren't worth the pain
of the seed infecting my brain

October 23

a war torn field
my heart is left razed
it can no longer yield
the warmth you once praised
the ground has been scorched
burned by hellfire
unwavering hands torched
my still breathing body upon its pyre
flames licked at my skin
turning it to molten glass
bathed in the heat on sin
I return to ash

birds soar overhead
I pray to fly together
but once I am dead
there's no blazing feather

October 24

can ash return to ember
once again turn aflame
I'm afraid I won't remember
the heat of passion's flame
in the middle of the night
when darkness brings cold
I've been left without a light
to see the world old

the past has left me
left me cold and alone
memory has lost the sea
and the way the stars above shone
above the water
above it all
I've brought myself to slaughter
to last breath's drawl

October 25

bellowing winds
are empty echoes
of the once fierce currents
I made my home
in the midst of golden fields
with storms blocking the sun
the end days have come
they've come for the deer
that grew fangs to fight
tired of running
tired of submission

nature has come
to undo what has been done
but how can you undo
that which still breathes?

I'll bite my tongue
while I still have teeth

October 26

setting sun
drowns me in rust
what's done is done
you can't return me to dust
I bare my teeth
forage no longer satiates me
I crave what hides beneath
the skin of those I see
living unaware
of the horrors I've lived
not knowing what it's like to bear
torture and then survived

there was no light at the end of the tunnel
I'm afraid we all return to dust

October 27

cyclical agony and ecstasy
wheels spin round
life drowned in fantasy
running feelings into the ground
through love and loss
I stand alone
only ever tossed
a measly bone
to stop my crying
stop the tears from my eyes
I lie here dying
clinging to promised lies

I stand alone
at the edge of everything and nothing
I no longer accept the bone
I accept resurrection and unbecoming

October 28

this end is final
I invoke rage primal
let this tether fall
from my mind tall
crash to the earth
- I wish for true rebirth

leave the phoenix behind
there is no ash
in my burning mind
only the pulsating gash
between soul and heart
keeping me separate
- tearing me apart

October 29

I cauterize my soul with my pyre
Wrath's flames fill me with hellfire
a life spent in melancholy
now the abyss calls out to me

I'm haunted by garlic mustard's memory
the scars in my mind have no remedy
there's no longer a place for me here
my end draws near
once again I'll fall to the sea
there will be nothing left of me
like a doe's corpse left in the sun
the buzzards will have their fun
as I'm reduced to bone
I will forever rest where garlic mustard's grown

October 30

let this diary be what's left of me
poetry's all I want to be
remembered by what I once loved
as these pages are shoved
beneath the coiled roots of that tree
which will evermore belong to me
unsullied by man's cruelty
as I become infinity

I will soar the skies above
as a beautiful dove
bringing peace to my kin
destroyed by the hands of sin

may this finality not be in vain
as my hopes and dreams
fall as purifying rain
for not all is as it seems

even the dead wish for peace

October 31

my time has come
to fate I succumb
I leave not in sorrow
but to find a better tomorrow
where the past is null
and no fear lives in my skull
a tomorrow where all this pain
is washed out with the rain

as I stand between the forest and sea
I realize what life could be
– but I cannot rewrite the past
so I pray this poem will be my last
with this final stroke of my pen
I free myself from a world of men
may this be the end of me
sincerely, Rosemary.

Acknowledgements

This book would not have been possible if not for those who have supported me along the way. Obviously, I was inspired to write by those who did not support me in the slightest, by those who deemed me lesser than them and treated me as such, but they deserve no acknowledgement. First and foremost, I would like to thank the women who came before me, the women who survived worse and thrived in spite of the world around them. The women who risked everything to travel to another continent in search of a better life for both them and their children. My ancestors have always inspired me, and I'm grateful to have inherited their grit. They've taught me to be an outspoken woman, to not be afraid to exist authentically in a world where our voices are taught to exist only in our heads, to never be afraid to pursue your passions, no matter what others have to say about it.

My mother raised me to speak my mind, and much to the chagrin of others, I always have and always will. While I wrote this book I was plagued with doubt, feeling that this would go nowhere, that I'm wasting time while I should be focusing on forging something more practical for myself. In these moments of doubt, I found myself thinking of a comment my mother once made; "if a man can do it, how hard can it *really* be?" I'm sure she's forgotten those words by now, but I also know if she were to read this, she'd throw her head back and laugh, agreeing wholeheartedly. I no longer remember the context of her words, but every time I see a man in the news being praised by millions, I think of her words, and envision myself in his place. She has supported me in all my creative endeavors as I have in hers. She taught me that it takes more than eyes to see the whole picture, that there's more to this world than just the physical. She inspires many of the female characters in my currently unfinished manuscripts. I'm forever grateful to have been raised in an environment where the veil between spiritual and physical was so thin, a place where my lived experience has proved time and time again that magic is not just in fairy tales.

The stories she's told me will always inspire me, and whenever I find myself thinking that I'm just like every other Joe Schmoe on the street, I think of her youth. She's experienced so much of what life has to offer, she's met so many interesting people, and every time I think she's run out of stories to tell me, she tells me something even more enthralling. Though I haven't always heeded her warnings, I will always go to her for advice, and for a good kvetch session.

I would also like to thank my father who taught me how to make a place for myself in this world, and even more importantly, to work for what I want. In the absence of any sons, I was raised in his image, raised on the stories of his youth and how he outgrew the environment he was raised in. I've always been inspired by how he managed to go from living in a trailer park in a small town almost no one has heard of, to landing a six figure job in the sunshine state. He turned nothing into something through nothing more than persistence and determination. I have big shoes to fill, and I pray he can fill them for decades to come, but when my time comes to pick up where he left off, I hope I can turn his legacy into something my own kids will write of in their own acknowledgements. Just as I think of my mother's words in times of doubt, I think of my father's own little phrases, Billisms, as we like to call them. While my mother and the mothers before her have taught me to persevere through times where all is against me, my father has taught me to laugh in the face of adversity, for the only thing that truly matters is staying true to yourself.

I heard of garlic mustard first in my high school conservation and field biology class. My teacher, Mr. Riley, was, and still is, incredibly passionate about the environment, always telling us how to identify invasive species and how to effectively remove them. Garlic mustard is, in plain English, a massive pain in the ass to get rid of. Simply pulling the roots out and tossing it isn't enough, you have to ensure not a single seed ever touches the ground, or the little pest would sprout up again. I remember spending countless hours picking it and crushing the flowers in my hand, the way I could never get the smell off my hands sickened me. Even if you do everything right, it will still spring up again. They create seed banks that hide in the dirt, waiting to sprout until the time is right. It could take decades to clear out a property overrun by it. Ever since Mr. Riley taught me how to identify it, I've seen it everywhere. On the bus ride home I'd see it on the side of every road, I'd see it on every walk, in every backyard. Inescapable. I hate it, and I always will, and this hatred is why I wrote this book. None of these pages would've been possible without Mr. Riley and his class, it was my favorite part of high school.

High school was where I finally realized the depths of my passion for writing. I took creative writing freshman year, and while I wasn't writing Shakespeare, I found pride in my work, in the drafts I still read in the hope I can fully realize them some day. That same year I found myself enamored by John Steinbeck's Of Mice and Men, I will forever love that book. Every time I throw myself into a writing project and devote myself to it in a manner bordering on manic, loving it so hard I can no longer sustain my adoration, burning myself out in a few chapters, I think of Lennie, loving that puppy so much he destroyed it. During both my junior and senior years, I took English with Mrs. Wryst, and though I still held onto my love of literature from my freshman year, I lost myself in it in her class. Reading Frankenstein fundamentally changed me as a person, I saw myself in Frankenstein's monster, and ever since then, I've strived to write a book in which at least one person feels seen in. Though I may never achieve the levels of recognition Mary Wollstonecraft Shelley did for her novel, I write in the hopes that I can encapsulate such an isolating experience so well that it inspires someone else out there to write their own books.

Mrs. Wryst helped me realize that my dreams were within reach, that I, too, could pursue writing as more than just a hobby. She taught me how to abuse a comma like there's no tomorrow, and use a semicolon like I actually know what it means. I will never forget a comment she left on one of my assignments; "You write quite well--you have many gifts. I hope you realize that." That one comment forever changed how I viewed my writing. I've always felt like a mediocre writer at best, but those words instilled me with the confidence I needed to write these poems. Though I know the first chapter or two might not live up to her expectations of me, I like to think of this book as me and Rosemary growing as poets together, the author evolving with their story. I cried when I realized I'd never have her class again, though my parents raised me, I believe Mrs. Wryst raised Stray B. Frankenstein.

 The year after, I was in a learning community at college, a little group of freshmen grouped by their major. I feel it's no surprise mine was psychology. We had little sharing circles every week, and I told them about my book. None of my peers really cared, but my professor loved that I was pursuing my passions. Shoutout Professor Ross.

Author's Note

As I write this, I feel this strange sense of
nostalgia, I never thought I'd get to realize this book.
It took me the better part of two years to finish this,
and it'll take me a lifetime to fully heal from the
events that inspired it. It feels strange to be in such a
different space both mentally and physically than I
was when I first began writing. For the first time in my
life, I'm not living in my hometown, I'm not
surrounded by the garlic mustard that inspired me.
My life has changed drastically since I first began
writing, I've left Appalachia behind for the beach, and
though I will return in the coming months, it
would've been unfathomable to the younger me that
I would ever leave. I feel like my life has become
Rosemary's and the sequel I dream of writing for her.

I almost abandoned this project for good, my
aspirations felt too lofty, too far out of the reach of my
small town hands. I've always dreamed of being an
author, and when I didn't immediately finish this
project as soon as I started, I was so discouraged I
nearly stopped writing for good. For as long as I can
remember, I've dreamed of seeing my books on
shelves, seeing people line up for a book signing,

being recognized for the blood, sweat, and tears I put into every word.

I hope this book reaches the right people, and I hope it helps me achieve my dreams of dedicating my life to my craft. One day, I hope this book and the ones that come after help me make a name for myself. Like Maya Lin and Joe Burrow, I pray I can put my talents to use and become more than just a kid from a town no one's ever heard of, and I pray this town will finally give Maya Lin the recognition it does Joe Burrow.

Thank you for reading this far, it means the world to me that someone cared enough to pick this book over millions of others, and enjoy it so much you took the time to read my rambling author's note. I hope my words inspired you to write a book of your own, and I hope that someday, somewhere out there, our books will be sold on the same shelf.

Poor Thing

Do you remember me? That poor girl in the back of the room. I was quiet, tame, a black sheep desperately trying to turn white. I remember the way you looked at me, nothing but pity. Pity in every eye I've ever met, it's sickening. Oh poor, helpless sheep, cursed to bear a life eternally ostracized. Poor thing, meant for a life beyond what you all imagined could possibly be. Loneliness drove me insane, crazed enough to dream, poor thing, dreams are for the wealthy. We are never meant to dream, cogs in the machine, poor thing needs a wake up call, or it'll end up begging on the corner, and we all know that's wrong. It's wrong to ask for such things, if you can't keep your life together, intact, how do we know you won't do it again? Undeserving, how dare you ask for that which you need, disappear from sight and never return, you're too raw for this world.

Poor thing wants to disappear, become so small, so delicately feminine, it turns to nothing. That's what women are meant for, poor thing dreams of more, dreams of indulging in what life has to offer without fear. Oh silly, stupid, thing! Dreams are for sleep, life cannot be a dream, you can be whatever you want as long as it's concrete, as long as every step has been made before. Walk in the same footsteps we all walk in, poor thing, you can't forge your own path. Success isn't guaranteed, your word does not yet hold value, keep your dreams under your pillow, or better yet, set your bed aflame, hope has corrupted your home.

Look to your father, practical, let him show you the light, darkness, you are supposed to bask in. Glory's light doesn't touch the downtrodden, hope has no place in the grand machine we were made for. Keep your eyes on the ground, little black sheep, surrender to the shepherd. I can't, I can't fit in the machine anymore, my dreams are too big for my body, and yet my wool still holds me captive. Won't you please shave me, dear shepherd? Let me roam on my own terms. Oh, poor thing, still believes in the divine, nothing can save you down here, God left this place long ago.

Heels click on the pavement, black skirt bellows in the wind. Poor thing, you stand out, do you not see the stares from those you've never met? Learn embarrassment, it's a college fad to explore the paths life has laid out for you. Wind picks up, black hair obscures your face, poor thing, how will you find a husband with your best asset hidden? Poor thing doesn't want a husband, foolish, women cannot provide for you like the wolves can.

Pushing the door open, a bell tolls, oh poor thing, why would you let them know you're here? Wolves stare from the corner of the room, depraved men, their captive sheep turn their heads up at you, too beautiful in your own right, a threat. With his teeth latched round your throat, he's greedy, setting his eyes on that which cannot be tame again. Poor thing, you know yourself too well, give into pressure, shed your clothes, soul, and put on something more fitting, simple. Wouldn't you look divine in bridal white?

The barista looks you up and down, poor thing braces for impact. Giggling, shedding your mask, you exchange compliments, black sheep are learning to flock

together. I wonder if her words are more than friendly, I

wonder if she, too, holds onto hope of never being a

wolf's trophy. Does she know we are free to choose

where our lives lead? Oh, poor thing, you have no

choice, one day you'll be made to see reality, you're

nothing more than flesh, your mind and the world within

holds no value when your body, flesh, is so beautiful,

ready for slaughter.